HENRY
THE SAILOR CAT

by Mary Calhoun & illustrated by Erick Ingraham

Morrow Junior Books

New York

To my sailing friends Pete, Robert, Marian, and Peter,
in gratitude for their help and tales of sailor cats
—M. C.

In memory of Serge Kehrli, and dedicated to all boating
enthusiasts who obey water safety rules
—E. I.

Watercolors were used for the full-color artwork. The text type is 17-point Garamond Light.

Text copyright © 1994 by Mary Calhoun. Illustrations copyright © 1994 by Erick Ingraham.

Printed in the United States of America.

2 3 4 5 6 7 8 9 10

Library of Congress Cataloging-in-Publication Data
Calhoun, Mary. Henry the sailor cat / by Mary Calhoun ; illustrated by Erick Ingraham.   p.   cm.
Summary: A stowaway cat proves his worth as a sailor during a sudden storm.
ISBN 0-688-10840-7.—ISBN 0-688-10841-5 (lib. bdg.)
[1. Cats—Fiction. 2. Sailing—Fiction.   3. Sea Stories.]   I. Ingraham, Erick, ill.   II. Title.
PZ7.C1278He 1994   [E]—dc20   92-29794   CIP   AC

Henry watched them put everything on the boat but him.

"Cats don't like water," The Man said. "Henry won't pester us to come sailing."

"No," said The Woman, "he'll stay with me."

Henry's tail lashed. Never mind water. What about going on the boat? What about the sea creatures they were always talking about, dolphins and whales? He wanted to see them.

As the boat motored off and The Woman called, "Don't forget to buy fuel," Henry slipped away. Past the smell of frying fish, he raced to the fuel dock.

While The Man and The Kid talked to the harbor master, Henry sprang aboard the sailboat. He saw a hatch propped open. Down the hatch went his paws, his ears, his tail. Henry hid.

Above, The Man called orders, sails were
hoisted, and sea gulls squalled. Below, Henry
crouched on an extra pile of sails that smelled
salty and damp. The water lapped gently, as if
it was stroking the boat. He felt the silent lift
of the craft as it carried him along.

Then the boat leaned with the wind and
the waves, and Henry's stomach leaned
with it.

He growled at his stomach. *Stop that!*
Switching his tail only made him feel sicker.
Air. He needed fresh air.

Henry padded through the cabin, up the
steps to the cockpit, and—

"Henry!" The Man cried. "How did you get on board? You'll fall in the ocean and drown."

"You stowaway!" The Kid laughed. "No, Henry's surefooted. He'll be a sailing Siamese."

Henry breathed the good brisk air. He rocked on his feet in time to the smooth bounding movement over the sparkling water. Now he felt *terrific*.

The Kid began to sing, "You're Henry the Sailor Cat." Henry joined in. "Meowy meow meow."

"Hmph!" said The Man. "Well, stay out of the way."

Henry scrambled up the wooden mast.
From the top, he could see everything. A
fishing boat passed, making for shore. Behind
it flew a cloud of hungry sea gulls. Channel
markers clanged; and black cormorants,
sitting on rocks, lifted their wings to dry them.

What a glorious day! Henry sniffed the cool breeze that riffled his whiskers and ruffled his fur. Gripping the mast, he swayed above the sea spread out below him.

"Yow-meow!" he cried in the joy of sailing.

Then Henry lurched as the boat turned
suddenly. He had to cling to keep from
falling. What! Going back already?
   "Good work," The Man told The Kid, who
held the tiller to steer the boat. "Now let's
practice that again."

The Kid cranked in a line to the forward sail.
The sail turned and the boat looped around again.
"Good," said The Man. "Now I'll show you
how to make the boat sail itself."

Henry saw The Man take a line tied to
the rail. He lashed it around the end of the
tiller with a slipknot. The Kid let go of the
tiller, and the boat sped along by itself.

"All right!" "Yow!"

"If you want to stop the boat, pull the
slipknot," The Man said.

"Like this?" The Kid pulled it loose.

Henry nearly flew off the mast as the boat turned into the wind and stopped, sails flapping noisily. The Man eased the tiller to the right and lashed it again as the boat sailed on.

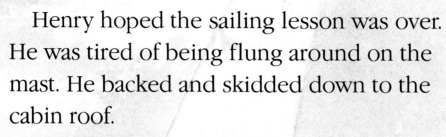

Henry hoped the sailing lesson was over. He was tired of being flung around on the mast. He backed and skidded down to the cabin roof.

"Hey, dolphins! Dolphins off the bow!" shouted The Kid.

Henry saw sleek creatures swimming close to the boat. Leaping in the water, they rode the bow waves.

On the cabin roof, Henry reared up to see better. He spread his back feet for balance.

The dolphins sprang up, too, arcing in dark-light rainbows over the water. Henry pranced, singing "Meowy meow meowl!" And the dolphins sang back in squeaks and whistles. "Clicky-whee!"

Now he had sea friends!

"I want to call to them!" The Kid exclaimed. "Where's my whistle?" He hurried to the stern and went below.

"Look, a whale is spouting!" The Man cried, leaning out over the rail.

In the distance Henry watched a great
hump roll in the water. He hissed in surprise
when a tail flipped up—and the whale was
gone.

"Looks like the weather's changing," The
Man muttered. "Storm clouds rolling in fast.
Better go back." He turned suddenly.
"Whoops!"

The Man slipped on the wet deck, and his
feet flipped up like the whale's tail as he went
over the side. The Man was gone!

No! He bobbed up in the waves, kept afloat by his life vest. "Help!" he called. The Man tried to swim toward the boat, but it kept moving farther away from him.

Henry raced to the cockpit. "Yowl!" The Kid couldn't hear him. What to do? Stop the boat! But how?

Then Henry remembered. He clawed at the line on the tiller. It wouldn't come loose. The boat sailed on. "Growl!" he rumbled, yanking again at the slipknot and digging in his claws.

The knot came untied and the boat stopped. Sails rattled.

At that The Kid rushed up the ladder. "What happened? Where's Dad?"

"Meowl!" Henry wailed, looking back to The Man. The wind was stronger, and the waves were higher.

"Dad!" The Kid screamed. "Oh, no!"

He seized the tiller. Carefully he brought the boat around.

Then he screamed again. "I can't see him!"
Where was he? Henry stood on his hind
legs, but he couldn't see The Man. He sprang
to the high side of the tilted boat. The deck
slanted so much that he had to struggle not to
slide as the boat bounced on the rolling
waves.

Way over there in the darkening water was
The Man.

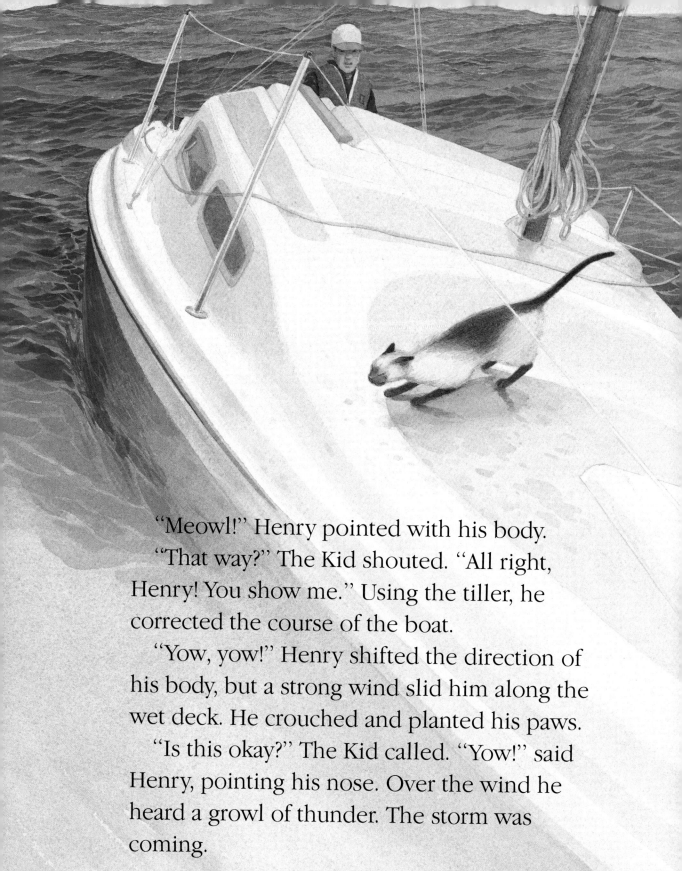

"Meowl!" Henry pointed with his body.

"That way?" The Kid shouted. "All right,
Henry! You show me." Using the tiller, he
corrected the course of the boat.

"Yow, yow!" Henry shifted the direction of
his body, but a strong wind slid him along the
wet deck. He crouched and planted his paws.

"Is this okay?" The Kid called. "Yow!" said
Henry, pointing his nose. Over the wind he
heard a growl of thunder. The storm was
coming.

"I see him! The waves are big, carrying him out," The Kid exclaimed. "The boat is tilting the wrong way. Got to be on his other side!"

As they passed The Man, The Kid shouted, "I'll get you!"

He tacked again. Henry ducked as water sprayed his fur.

"Sorry!" The Kid gasped. "Now where?"
"Yowl!" Henry pointed.
The Kid steered close to The Man, turning
the boat into the wind. The sails shook, and
the boat's speed slowed to a drift.

"Coming!" The Man yelled. He swam
toward the boat.

Quickly The Kid put down the swim ladder. The Man reached for it, but the boat rocked away. "Mew." Henry stood as near the low rail as he dared.

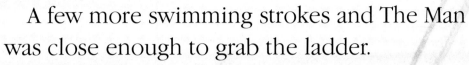

A few more swimming strokes and The Man
was close enough to grab the ladder.
   He struggled onto it and heaved himself
over the rail into the boat. "Whew!" he
gasped, flopping on a seat.

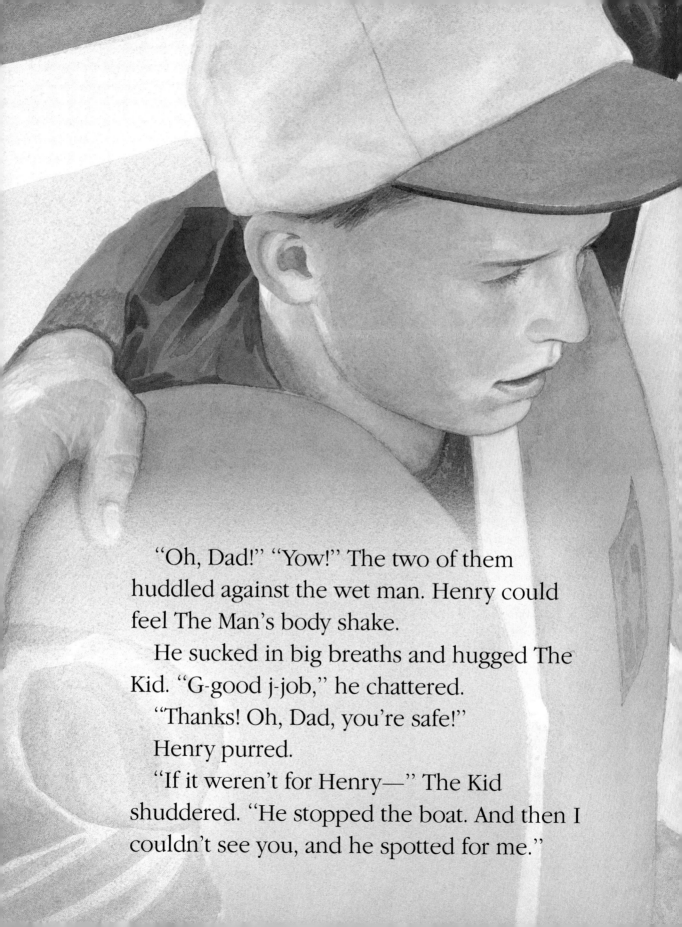

"Oh, Dad!" "Yow!" The two of them
huddled against the wet man. Henry could
feel The Man's body shake.

He sucked in big breaths and hugged The
Kid. "G-good j-job," he chattered.

"Thanks! Oh, Dad, you're safe!"
Henry purred.

"If it weren't for Henry—" The Kid
shuddered. "He stopped the boat. And then I
couldn't see you, and he spotted for me."

"Henry, you good crew mate! Thank you!
I'm glad you stowed away!"
The sound in The Man's voice made Henry
purr with happiness.

"How'd you fall in?"
"Tell you later," said The Man, getting up to lower the mainsail. "Now we've got to race for the harbor before the storm breaks!"

The Man started the engine and the motor
whined.

Henry swayed on his feet while the boat
bucked the waves. Scrambling up to the bow,
he saw a row of dolphins arch out of the
water, leading the way. He knew they'd make
it. Some smart sailing Siamese!